50 Miles

The journey backward

50 MILES

THE JOURNEY BACKWARD

JAYDEEP KHOT

Kalamos Literary Services LLP

Kalamos Literary Services LLP
Email: info@kalamos.co.in | editorial@kalamos.co.in

Published in 2018
by
Kalamos Literary Services
ISBN- 978-93-87780-19-4

Typeset in Kalamos Literary Services LLP

Illustrations done by Prasun Balasubramaniam

Dedicated to
my four pillars of strength.
My father, Surendra Khot
My mother, Puja Khot
My maternal grandmother, Sheela Samant
My sister, Tanvi

INTRODUCTION

This story revolves around the life of Haria. Haria is a 50-year-old man, who has amnesia. He doesn't even remember his name. The story will take you, into the journey of his life in reverse chronological order. Here, the central character of the book finds clues, which help him recall his life. Each clue would help him remember a year at a time.

So, join Haria, in his journey of self-revelation *50 Miles*, where he embarks upon his identity, origin, and place of birth.

PROLOGUE

I woke up with a jolt. I looked out of the window; it was still dark outside. The clock on the wall showed it was 3:15 am. I realised that I have woken up from a nightmare. A nightmare like no other. My hands trembling and my eyes wide open. My beard was itchy. I picked up my Scotch from the right of the table and gulped it. A sudden sound startled me, and I turned around, with cold sweat trickling down my spine. I soon realised it was the doorbell. I wondered who it would be at the door at this unearthly hour. My heart still pounding, I walked to the door and reluctantly opened it. There was nobody at the door. I looked around and could not see anybody.

As I was about to close the door, my eyes fell on an envelope that lay on the doormat. It was addressed to 'Haria'. I was lost in my thoughts. I had this irresistible urge to open the envelope to see the contents. My rational mind argued against the thought. I asked myself, "How can I open somebody's private letter?"

My inquisitive mind wanted the opposite to happen.

I kept the envelope on the table, as my mind debated whether I should open the envelope or not.

My dilemma aggravated as time passed by.

As I faced the dilemma, for an unknown reason, I tried to reflect upon my life and was shocked that I couldn't recollect a thing. Initially, I thought I was yet to be wide awake from my deep slumber. But that was not the case; I realised that I did not know who I was. My mind was blank. I felt that the brightness of the day would remove the darkness of my mind.

AGE 50

The clock struck six, and I could see the sunrise, bringing with it the brightness of the day and pushing the dark night out. I had spent three hours introspecting myself and was still in dark about who and where I was.

The letter seemed to be the only ray of hope for me to be enlightened about myself and I decided to open the envelope. It dawned upon me now that the letter was addressed to 'Haria'.

The letter read:

Dear Honey,

Wish you a very happy birthday, Sweetie! I hope this golden jubilee year brings more clarity in your life. Have been missing you of late. Sorry, couldn't come to meet you personally. I have sent your favorite Flister's Scotch. Enjoy it to the last sip. Xoxo.

Regards
Kasak

My hands went cold and numb after reading the words 'Flister's Scotch'. During this tense moment, I knew only Scotch would give me solace and rushed to see the bottle of Scotch, from which I drank the previous night.

I read the label on the Scotch bottle aloud, "Flister's Scotch".

What a coincidence! Whoever this Haria was, we shared a common interest—Flister's Scotch.

I quickly swigged the alcohol from the bottle in my hand. I could feel the Scotch travel through my veins to the brain.

The alcohol probably opened my mental faculties, and it dawned upon me that I was in a one bedroom-hall-kitchen apartment, owned by someone named 'Haria' and the bottle, from which I had gulped Scotch last night, was his birthday gift from his loved one.

"But who am I?" I wondered. My brain was flooded with questions about my relationship with Haria. Was I his friend, brother, cousin, son…Who was I? I knew Haria or somebody else in the house would be able to answer my questions. In a couple of minutes my search for any human presence in the house was over. There was nobody else in the house, except me. That realization added to my discomfort as my questions remained unanswered. I felt claustrophobic in the house and rushed out to get a whiff of fresh air.

The freshness of the morning air seemed to have brought about some clarity in mind. I felt silly that it did not strike me to ask my neighbours about Haria.

Their response to my query was disheartening. Each of my neighbour ridiculed me for asking about Haria and banged the door on my face. I was disappointed, but I am not the one to give up so easily. I gathered courage to meet the lady, who had sent the letter. She was my only hope to learn about Haria, and that was to be a clue to my being.

Luckily for me, she had mentioned her address on the letter, making it easy for me to track her down.

I went to that address and rang the doorbell. An elderly woman opened the door.

When she saw me, her eyes filled with tears and she hugged me saying, "Haria, I knew you would come to meet me on your birthday!" Her statement came as a shock, yet it gave me my identity. So, I was Haria! No wonder, the neighbours laughed at me when I asked them for details of Haria.

I asked her, "How am I related to you?"

She replied, "I'm your ex-girlfriend."

Out came another question from me, "Since when are we dating?"

She answered, "Since a year."

Then I probed her about our dating experience.

I guess that was the stupidest mistake that I made since I understood my identity, because, my probe started her blabbering, which I felt was stupid.

I had no option but to listen to it thinking it to be true; so, I listened to her.

It was crucial for me to listen to her. Her voice was musical to me. As I got lost in her musical voice, I did not realise that she was being sceptical about my auditory faculties. I was brought back to the reality of listening to her, when I heard her shout, "Are you listening to me?"

"Yes, madam," I muttered.

In a raised voice, she asked like a school teacher, "OK. Now tell me, what did you hear?"

Initially, I stammered but regaining my confidence, I started talking.

The words from my mouth flew like birds from the nest. I said 'blah blah blah blah.'

She became very emotional and said, "You don't have to be scared Haria. You need to relax. Calm down please."

Then I gathered myself and said in a low voice, "I didn't hear a single word of what you said."

She said, "It's ok. I'm repeating all that I said."

Then there was a battery of words from her. "I said you have harassed me," she shouted.

Gathering courage, I asked her, "Are you sure?"

"Yes! Of course," she replied.

"Please enlighten me. How did I harass you?" I said.

I was shattered when I heard her say that I took physical advantage of her.

I was shocked and scared. My hands trembled. My mouth was wide open as she told me that she gave me a heart attack.

"What nonsense!" I said in astonishment.

"Yes, yes," she retorted.

Wanting to know more about what I could have done, "What next? Please tell me? What else happened?"

She asked me in annoyance, "Isn't this enough?"

I said, "Please tell me, I don't even remember a thing dear." She giggled and said, "Ok, listen, but calm down, before I speak, you need to mentally prepare yourself for this."

I was nervous and trembled with fear. "OK," I muttered.

I was self-conscious as I looked at her wide-open eyes.

I assumed to adopt the pessimistic approach as I approached her.

It was something very unnatural.

As I approached her, I smelt foul odour emitting from her mouth. The odour was coupled with that of Four-Square cigarette.

I guess I had a nervous breakdown from that smell.

Her figure looked like that of a character from the video game Penguin of Madagascar.

Suddenly she said, "Listen, all that was a joke!"

I heaved a sigh of relief on hearing that.

She said, "You have always been a really nice guy."

That gave me a sense of satisfaction. I told her, "You're extremely fiendish."

She gave me a wicked smile and said, "You are generic.'

I felt that my thoughts were still blocked because of the scotch I had last night and in the morning.

My eyes felt heavy. She came close to me, held my chin up and said, "Listen, carefully! I always thwarted the idea of falling for you, but my heart always guided me towards you. Your brain was devoid of intelligence, and you always ignored those who censured you. That my dear was something very prolific. I fell for your charisma."

Startled by what she said, I sat up on my seat and listened to her.

I was mesmerised.

She told me that I wasn't a cliché.

"Sometimes you became grumpy.

But I did fart and make you laugh.

But I often saw a cleft in you."

"You would never talk whenever I asked you about your previous year. You always used to look at this keychain," saying this she opened a box.

Watching her in the act, I asked, "Is this the Pandora's box?"

She said in a loud voice, "Get out of your mediocrity. It is time to come out of your safe harbour and listen carefully!"

Instinctively, I felt that she would start bickering and I prepared myself for the situation.

"You told me that she is ok, isn't she?"

I asked, "What? Where is your blabbering going?'

In my subconscious mind, I understood that I used the wrong word and that was 'blabbering'.

My words were followed by a staccato of abuses from her. The words started hitting my heart like some stones thrown by a beggar on my car.

"Do you think that I am stupid?" she retorted.

I replied, "No, madam. I was drunk last night that's why I used the wrong word."

"What do you mean by wrong? It was insulting."

I gathered courage and apologised to her. "I'm sorry, Kasak," I said. She then opened the box and showed me the keychain that she had mentioned.

On the keychain was engraved *Bandra*.

Seeing the keychain and the reading the word Bandra, there was a muddle of thoughts in my mind. Bandra was familiar. This suburb of Mumbai seemed to be telling me something. On the one hand, I felt it was trivial, but on the other hand, I felt there was much to it. I was left dumbstruck. A flashback so real as if it was actually happening to me.

My brain said it was trivial.

But it also said that it was chronic and needed to be treated.

So, I started looking at it carefully, and it obscured my vision.

The keychain read the same words 'BANDRA.'

Which left me spellbound.

AGE 49

I waved Kasak a goodbye and embarked on my journey to Bandra.

It was a very hectic journey.

There I saw big bungalows.

The bungalows were huge, but the inhabitants had a melancholic look on their faces.

My eyes fell on a woman, with hair cluttered. She had a cigarette in her right hand, while her left hand was on her hip.

I presumed that she had a backache.

Her eyes became small.

And I thought she was introspecting.

Introspecting about the hideous crimes she had done, the favours she had taken to live in that bungalow.

I decided to take my mind off the lady and the bungalow and to concentrate on the journey ahead.

Only one word haunted me, and that was 'Bandra'. I looked at the road ahead. A bus stop drew my attention, where people were running for a bus. Their legs seemed to have the strength of a horse.

Their personalities were stern.

Their eyes were full of aspirations.

Near the bus stop, I saw children from the slums.

Educated youth were conducting a class for these children on the pavement near the bus stop. I felt that the children were keen on taking informal education and acquiring skills that would help them take care of their basic needs of food and shelter.

It struck me that the cost of teaching was being borne by some old people. I wondered why they were donating their earnings for the purpose. Did they believe that their donation would act like a swash to wash away the sins they may have committed?

Questions kept cropping up in my mind. "Were these elderly people paedophilic?" I immediately brushed off that question. I realised that my mind was corrupt to have such thoughts. The answer to my question was right in front of me. It was a big, NO.

These children were gems – gems of India, who were lying in the slums, without the society realising their value.

Sooner or later they would come out of their situation, with degrees from good colleges.

With their earnings, they would feel like kings and would take care of their parents with royalty, though their parents could not provide them with basic facilities for a decent life.

The children were mature enough to understand that their parents had provided them all that they could within their means.

The children wore tattered clothes and their bodies and clothes emitted a foul smell, which came from the absence of regular bath coupled with low personal hygiene level.

The high-class people maintained a distance from them presuming that they might catch some infection from these dirty and unhygienic children.

But then I saw something positive. There were signs of hope on the faces of the children's parents, who came to take them home.

They carried in their hearts a dream of seeing a different India, where children growing up in the slums end up in top positions in corporate organisations, wearing formal clothes.

Suddenly, I was back to reality.

In front of me was a poor man sweeping the street. I stood there and observed him. While carrying out his task of cleaning the road, he would occasionally glance at the students attending the roadside class. There was a sparkle in his eyes, as he saw a little girl learning the English alphabets in that class.

My eyes fell on the girl, and to my surprise, she resembled Kasak.

She asked her teacher, "*A ke baad B kyu aata hai?*" (Why does B follow A?)

The teacher was dumbstruck. No student had asked such a question all these years. Impressed by the girl's question, the sweeper had a smile on his face, as if he was her father.

The teacher jumped off his seat looked at the sky and made an obscure movement of his hands and said, "A stands for Apple."

From the corner of his eye, he observed the girl as she wrote the letter 'A' in her notebook; she wrote the letter reversely, going from right to left. It was then that he realised that the girl was dyslexic and a fantabulous idea struck him. He thought he should tell the girl a story and started telling her a story of a boy who was very hungry.

The girl showed interest in the story; the reason being that she was also very hungry.

Food was the only incentive for her to be here.

This was the story:

There was a boy who was very hungry. So, he got an apple 'seb'. (*Seb* is apple in Hindi.) So 'A' for apple.

So, then he became hungry, so he fetched for a ball, thus B for 'Ball.'

The girl developed more interest in the story and was curious to hear further.

She didn't even realise that she farted in the intensity of knowing what's going to happen next.

The teacher continued: While playing, he saw a cat running. "Why was the cat running?" asked the little girl.

The teacher said, "Before that, I want to tell C is for Cat."

She understood and listened. The teacher continued:

The cat was running because a dog was chasing her.

So here what did we understand? D for Dog.

The girl could imagine the entire scenario.

The teacher continued:

Bigger than the dog is the elephant. Therefore, E for Elephant.

The girl started dancing because she was awestruck by the story.

As I watched this beautiful scenario, I turned around and looked at the sweeper. He was crying. The tears were like those of a proud father, seeing his daughter learn English. I walked up to the sweeper and gave him a handkerchief to wipe his tear. "Why are you taking so much interest in that little girl, is she your daughter," I asked curiously.

Wiping his eyes with the handkerchief given by me, he said, "No, I have adopted her. She was abandoned with a letter kept by her side."

The frail man took out a crumpled piece of paper from his pocket. "This was left by her side. I carry it with me every day," the sweeper told me handing it over to me.

He asked me to read the letter, stating that he is illiterate.

There were only five words on the piece of paper, but those words froze me. I was shocked, as I read the five words in disbelief: Regards from Kasak and Haria.

Several questions came to my mind. Why does the letter have Kasak's name and mine? Was she our daughter? Was I the father?

I felt a sudden pain in my heart and guilt in my mind. What have I done? How could my daughter be left on the street?

I walked up to the girl and lifted her to make her stand on the bench. I now found her to be prettier and noticed that she had lovely pink skin.

Her innocent smile, her eyes, and her gestures reminded me of Kasak.

I asked this girl, "Do you know me?"

She stared at me. With a twinkle in her eyes and a lisp, she said, "You look like the uncle, who used to play with me." That one sentence was enough to traumatise me. If she is my daughter, what a grave sin I have committed, I thought. Were there more sins committed by me? A long list of possible sins flooded my mind.

To me, the voice of this eight-year-old girl was like that of Kasak's.

Her story left me mesmerised. Her story was strange, and it was like that of Kasak's. She too started telling me her story in reverse chronology.

AGE 47

The little girl's story.

I am currently eight years old.

This entire year I spent learning, and I started going to a municipal school and have been learning there.

She pointed her fingers towards the sweeper and said, "He is my super-cute dad."

The sweeper had an awkward smile on his face.

She looked down and said that this year was tough. I put a hand on her shoulder, but she immediately shrugged and in a raised voice said, "Don't try to harass me sexually."

There was a pain in her eyes. I noticed that she had bruises on her hand.

She threw a glance at me and told me not to show her any false sympathy.

I understood what went inside her.

Her past was like an open book.

An open book full of sexual harassments and assaults.

I looked down at my feet and was about to get up, but she held my hand and said in a low voice, "You need to listen to me."

I asked her, "But why should you tell me? You do not even know me?"

She answered, "Yes, you are right."

"Then why do you wish to tell me?' I asked.

"Because you look like the uncle I had seen some years ago."

I agreed to listen to her story.

I could then understand that this eight-year-old girl saw me as a father figure.

I realised that I was obliged to sit by her side and listen to her diligently.

She started narrating her story. It was like poetry to my ears, yet her story caused me great pain, as it was a tragic story.

"When I was 7 years old this man, who is sweeping the floor called me to his slum.

He told me he had chocolates and showed them to me.

The names of those chocolates were m&m's, Snickers and Mars.

I flipped the chocolates and saw that the MRP was too high; extremely high, which obviously the sweeper couldn't afford."

Such thoughtfulness is seen even in this poor girl, but found to be lacking in the elite class, I thought.

The elite class also knew that such expensive chocolates were not affordable to the sweeper.

A rich person may have thought that the sweeper had stolen those chocolates from the nearby store. But that was not the case.

The sweeper had saved money over a couple of months to buy those chocolates for this little girl.

As he was handing the chocolates to the little girl, their hungry neighbour attacked the sweeper with a stick, with the intention of snatching the chocolates and consuming them.

This led to a scuffle between the sweeper and the neighbour, but it left the little girl hurt.

While continuing her story, the girl had an innocent smile on her face. She said, "I learnt a lesson from this uncle."

"What?" I asked.

She replied, "Rich things make people poor."

I looked into her eyes. They displayed pain; inexplicable pain.

"I spent an entire year looking at marks left by the bruises while this man used to go about his task of sweeping the streets."

I started at her bruise marks.

She then pointed to the sweeper, wanting me to look at him.

I turn around to look at him. On looking at him, I felt that he wanted to say something.

"Yes, what do you wish to say?" I asked him.

"I love my job, I really love my job," he said.

I curiously asked, "Why?"

Looking at his book with reverence he said, "As I sweep, I clean the dirt off the streets and sometimes wish this even clears the dirt in the minds of my fellow Indians."

"Such a simple man and such great thoughts,"
I felt.

I understood that my developing country had scope for improvement because of these people, who had such a spectacular mind frames despite being so poor.

AGE 46

The story continues with a twist, a twist like no other.

The girl stopped talking and looked at an Audi that stopped nearby.

A fair boy in a dark suit came out of his car. He gave her an evil grin.

She became uncomfortable and held my hand. I could sense fear running through her heart. She was scared, extremely scared.

The Richie-rich lad then went back to his car and drove off.

I asked her, "Are you alright?"

"Yes. Of course, I'm," she said.

I said, "Why did you stop blabbering then?"

'Oh god, I again said that word,' I said to myself.

"Please continue," I told her.

"Let me take a deep breath first," she told me.

Five minutes went by, but it looked like a long wait, and once again she started the course of her story.

She continued, "I'm six years old now. A person identical to you taught me how to smile; showed me the ocean; explained to me why the ocean was blue; he taught me to jump; to be an independent person; about good and bad touch by a man; and taught me to be a good human being."

I did not realise, that while listening to her story, I started crying.

"Please go on," I said. "Please go on," I repeated. I was keen on knowing what happened next.

She stared at me.

I asked her, "Why are you staring?"

She exclaimed, "You are mad!"

I said, "No. Why! Any rational person would ask, 'what happens ahead?'"

She showed me a straight face and told me, "I already told you before, can't you recall?"

Saying this, she hit me on my forehead.

That knock on the head immediately made me remember everything.

I was very curious about this reverse story.

I asked her, "Why are you telling me your story backwards?"

She replied, "Because I like to tell the best things in the end."

Best things.

Those words made me wonder.

Even the best things in the world have depressed people.

AGE 45

She continued, at age 6.

There was a younger version of you, with a beautiful woman. You both would come here. I remember seeing you run, hold hands, kiss each other on the cheeks and pull each other's cheeks.

I remember your younger self calling out, "Kasak, Kasak look. Isn't this beautiful?"

Kasak would ask, "What?"

You would point at me and say, "See, isn't our creation cute?"

Kasak's eyes would wide open.

"'Hush,' she said"

"You shouted 'She should know right?'"

"Kasak looked down and said

"'It's better that she doesn't know it.'"

"When both of you stared, I dug myself in my book and started studying again.

It was a cold December. You both got me gifts; sweaters, pens, pencils, notebooks, and textbooks.

The affection in your eyes, gave me the comfort and warmth of a home, though I was on the streets of Bandra.

While both of you ran, I was learning to walk.

When I heard the 'I love you' words from your mouth, I understood that there are better words in the oxford dictionary.

You were a wonderful pair. Sleeping on the benches of Carter Road, I always dreamt of the two of you. Both of you would appear in my dreams."

'Lovely creatures' was the only thing which was going on in my mind.

She stopped, and I realised that my heart was full of joy. I felt like a father talking to his daughter.

On that street I found my freedom; the freedom to find a loved one; a part of my soul; a part of me left on the streets to rot.

Soon I realised that I was here for a purpose, but I was getting very emotionally attached to the girl, whose name, I didn't even know. So, I asked her name.

She replied in one of the softest voices in the world.

"Nazuk," she said.

'Such a co-incidence,' I thought.

AGE 44

Borborygmus.

Borborygmus.

Even in the noise of traffic and honking of horns by motorists, I heard the girl's borborygmus.

"Are you hungry?" I asked.

"No. Are you stupid?" she queried.

"No," I said.

She stood up and pointing to her stomach and said, "My intestines are cleaning themselves."

"Oh!" I said.

"She is my daughter, the smartest," I thought to myself.

She smiled.

"Don't be an eccedentesiast," I stated.

She got agitated and simply walked off. I followed her and held her hand.

"Tell me about you when you were five years old. The journey is going backwards right?" I said.

She looked at me through the corner of the eye and said, "You don't seem to be interested in listening to my story."

I shook her hands rigorously.

"Please sit down and tell me your story. I am too keen on listening to it!" I exclaimed.

"One day, when I was five-years-old," she started blabbering, "You and Kasak were arguing over which ice-cream to give me.

Kasak's favourite was mango, and your favourite was elaichi.

Both of you continued your argument, with Kasak holding an elaichi flavoured ice-cream and you holding mango flavoured.

As both of you struggled to feed me, the ice-creams fell on the floor."

"A dog in the manger attitude. *Tula Nahi Mala Nahi Ghal Kutarayala,*" Kasak shouted at the top of her voice, and you looked at me and did an obscure movement to close my ears.

"I guess she was saying something really bad. Something that children of my age shouldn't hear."

I realised that this girl was brilliant, extraordinarily brilliant. That thought kept ringing in my mind, until the snapping of fingers by this girl stopped it, bringing me back to reality. Her eyes said that she had plenty of more to tell. The backward journey was yet to be completed.

She said, "Do you want to hear about age four?"

My voice trembled as I said,

"Yes."

AGE 43

"So here comes the best part," she said.

I couldn't control my curiosity, yet waited for the climax.

The golden words flew from her mouth, which said, "You both aren't my biological parents. At age four, I saw two poor people arguing with the two of you. They claimed to be my biological parents."

That statement left me shocked, as I pondered over it.

I started sweating from my forehead as if I had done a workout. I had never done any work out in the past; that is what I felt. Even if I had, I didn't remember it.

But yes, my bulging belly was a clear sign that I had never exercised.

My ribs seemed to settle on my stomach when I sat down. And I ate till the food refused to go down from my throat.

The delivery boy from McDonald's served me all my meals daily.

'McDonald's.'

The burger and my tummy looked identical, I felt. The little girl giggled as I was lost in my thought, it was as if she read my mind.

'My daughter, after all, though not my biological one,'
I sighed.

AGE 42

The story continued like a movie. It touched my soul, and I wanted to know more. I was curious; extremely curious.

"Please tell me more. Please," I begged of her with my voice raised.

My raised voice attracted the attention of all those on Carter Road--the pedestrians, the joggers, the beggars, as well as the street children were playing cards.

She continued as she giggled.

When I was three-years-old, you were 81 kgs. You wore a Santa Claus dress, and you came to impress me.

"I somehow, knew that you had come for me," the girl told me shyly, and I laughed looking at my stomach.

I realised that at three years of age, the child knew so much about life.

As I diligently heard her speak, my heart sank, as if in a deep ocean, from which it was difficult to get out.

AGE 41

"Age 2! Age 2!" I shouted.

Everybody looked at me again. The girl stood up from her seat and shouted back, "Are you mad?"

I trembled in my seat.

I asked, "Why? What happened?"

She taunted me saying, "You don't remember the events in your life, and you expect me to remember what happened when I was two years old! Get lost."

Those words pinched my heart. She was telling me to get lost from the street; the street where she was raised.

"You abandoned me, you stupid fool." She put her hand in the pocket and removed a letter, which stated:

"I'm sorry for abandoning you, dear daughter.
I will come for you one day. That day, give me this letter, and it will remind me how cruel I was".

My hands trembled.
I felt atelophobic.
As I flipped, the letter it had an address of Hiranandani Business Park.
I immediately rushed for an autorickshaw and asked the driver to start.
"Why are you so agitated brother?" he asked.
Such great command over the language, I wondered.
As I sat on the autorickshaw, I looked at the little girl; she was weeping. I wanted to wipe her tears.
But I knew that I couldn't wipe the sorrow from her soul.

AGE 40

The autorickshaw driver speeded up his vehicle, making me feel that I was in an Audi.

"Perfectionist," I thought!

With all the events that happened in the past few hours, I felt the mental fatigue. As a result, I quickly fell asleep and woke up when the autorickshaw driver announced, "*Uth Jao Bhaiya Hiranandani Aa Gaya.*" (Get up brother, we are at Hiranandani.)

Right in front of me was The Cream City'.

"I might have cherophobia" I heard a fat girl saying.

When I saw her, she looked at me as if I had committed a crime.

I read the address, which was written on the back of the letter.

I asked plenty of people for the address, but each of them misguided me.

I sat down on a bench and looked at my toes.

Apparently, I was fooled by a street girl. I had this sudden urge to gulp some Scotch.

I opened my flask and gulped some Scotch.

A man walking down the street looked at me, stopped and called out, "Haria?????"

I immediately stood up from my seat and said, "You know me?"

He said, "Yes, of course. I know you would come," he replied, adding "Let's have a chat in my office, Harish."

I followed him as he walked fast. I tried to maintain the same pace, but I wasn't able to. He was too fast.

"What is your age?" I asked him.

"Does it matter?" he retorted.

Before I realised we were at his office. I felt like being in heaven. The place was heavenly.

The office had flowers of a variety of colours, giving out beautiful soft fragrance.

"Please, have a seat. It has been a long time since I met you. How have you been?" he asked.

He looked me in my eyes as if he looked into my soul. I tried to hide my eyes from him.

He shouted, "Don't hide your eyes; it shows a sense of insecurity."

I immediately looked at him in the eye, as if fixing it to an object., "Don't stare so much that will make me feel uncomfortable," he smiled as he said this.

"Ok," I said.

"So, what brings you to Hiranandani?" he asked inquisitively.

"To remember my past," I said in a low voice.

He laughed, and he fell on the floor.

"Rofl rofl rofl." He said.

"Are you ok?" he said.

I was shocked.

Stammering and impatient.

"What do you want to know?" he asked.

"My past," I repeated.

He said, "Ok," and got up from his chair and drew a big man on a whiteboard. The drawing was too big to fit on the board.

"Why such a big man?" I asked him.

"Why?" I repeated impatiently.

"You were a big man" he smiled.

"Then what happened?" I asked him curiously.

"You fell in deep love. The deepest love possible. You drowned in love. You were at the height of your career, but love brought you down."

"You started visiting doctors, your business went on for a toss, your employees left you. Your parents and your siblings also left you, because your heart was vested in a girl."

"Your investments showed nil returns, because you, the mastermind fell in deep love." and he started laughing once again.

An obvious question cropped up in my mind. I knew he had the answer for it and I was eager to know it, yet was scared to hear, wondering what was in store.

"What was the girl's name?" I asked.

"Reshma," he announced.

"What?" I asked in astonishment.

"Are you sure?" I asked and repeated my query,

"Are you sure?"

"Yes, of course," he said.

"You have a doubt?" he questioned.

"No," I said.

"You had a zero-bank balance, my boy," he laughed.

He gave me an address.

"Go meet her," she will tell you the rest of your forgotten story.

He closed his eyes and took a deep breath.

"Go here she will be waiting for you. Nice meeting you, you have done us many favours, you can never be forgotten, you will always be in my heart," he said.

"Are you gay?" I asked.

"Does it make a difference?" he reciprocated.

"No," I said.

"Then why did you ask?"

"Harish, please leave."

As I was getting up from my chair, he muttered, "Please leave, please leave."

I understood, I told him. I stood up, turned around to leave and did not look back. I heard him laugh. I knew that it would hurt me if I turned to look at him. I lightly closed the door behind me.

His laughter was like a hyena; it continued to haunt me.

My mind was blank; there seemed to be a blackout.

I looked at the address, and it read:

Resham, Andheri. Blackout and Andheri"

What a coincidence, I thought.

AGE 39

It was midday, I rubbed my eyes, yawned, and burped after eating a delicious pizza on the way.

I was stuck in a traffic jam, and there was too much of honking.

It made my head burst with fear.

I was gripped with fear; fear of being unknown; of being forgotten; of forgetting everything; of understanding who I really was?

It sent a shiver down my spine.

"Reshma, Reshma" were the voices I heard in my mind.

"*Andheri mein andhakar hain,*" somebody shouted from behind.

The taxi driver abused him and honked as much as he could.

I wondered if this honking could make us fly. I could run faster than that I thought.

As the taxi moved at snail's speed, I introspected my life; my journey of finding myself; exploring myself; understanding whether I was a monster or a devil. Whether I had been a good man or a bad one. Whether I had committed sins or had virtues.

These questions needed answers.

I scanned the nook and corner of Andheri for five hours non-stop but to my disappointment.

I enquired with a large number of people but, nobody knew about Reshma. Then suddenly, I saw a saree shop named *The Reshma Shop*. I thought this was what that runner wanted me to go for.

I hesitantly entered the shop.

With the crowd and the noise inside, it was more like a fish market.

"*Do Saree 15,000 rupayee ki. Teen saree li toh uspe ek sadi free,*" somebody was screaming.

"Fish market!" I thought to myself and wondered what I was doing there. "Hey, Tondu! Come here," a lean man called out to me from behind a counter.

I made a quick move towards him, but while doing so bumped into two elderly women.

The women were obviously furious as one of them gave me a tight slap and the other showered abuses on me I was surprised by the strength of the woman who slapped me and the vocabulary of the one who abused.

I felt like a rapist.

Some neighbourhood serial killer.

"Harish, I knew you would come. So fatso, what brings you here?" he asked.

"How do you know me?" I asked with a sense of urgency.

"You used to come here with a super cute girl," he replied.

"Oh!" I exclaimed.

"Can you name here?" I asked.

"Rupa," he said.

"Both of you would always argue at the top of your voices on the choice of saree and which one would look better on her, drawing the attention of all those in the shop and throwing the shop in silence, but for your voices," he stated.

When you two used to bicker.

"Bangles, Bangles, Bangles"

"I want the yellow bangles,

No, wait I want the green bangle."

"No, no, no, the black one, I want."

"When you used to take the black one.

She used to quarrel for the white one.

You both used to come here,

Literally every day.

You had an aura, a charisma, of your own.

A sense of love and belonging you guys had.

You both knew the soul of each other very well.

It seemed like it was one soul."

"Are you a philosopher or a saree seller?" I asked.

"Both," he replied and started laughing.

"Where can I find Rupa?" I asked him, eagerly wanting to meet Rupa.

"Jogeshwari," he said.

AGE 38

My journey continued; this time from Andheri to Jogeshwari, a short distance indeed.

Suddenly, I felt lonely. The solitude is indescribable.

The word Rupa kept ringing on my mind.

I alighted from the autorickshaw, which brought me to Jogeshwari. After paying the fare, I looked at the sky and shouted, "Rupaaaa," oblivious that I was at a public place.

I wished for a miracle to happen and that miracle was to meet Rupa.

Rupa, Rupa, Rupa, Rupa, that was the only thought on my mind.

Though I could not recollect her face, in the hope of finding her, I looked out for her all around me. Once again I looked up in the sky, calling out her name, and suddenly an aircraft caught my attention. I was surprised to read the name on it, "Rupa Airlines".

Like a madman, I started running in the direction of the flight, as if to catch up with the aircraft. I stumbled and fell down after two steps. I was not watching my steps, instead, I was looking at the sky.

I fell to the ground, making me feel that one should not look up so high that one forgets one's roots.

A man lent me a helping hand to get up.

"So finally, you came back? Didn't you?" he asked me.

"You know me?" I reciprocated.

"Who doesn't?" he questioned and said, "Let's have a chat at my place," he said.

I followed him to his place, which was in a chawl, but he addressed it as his palace.

He offered me a rickety chair to sit, and I sat down. The chair collapsed due to my weight, putting me on the floor. He started laughing. "Hariaaaaa, you still haven't changed."

"I don't remember anything," I said.

I asked him what had happened to me.

"Wait, I will tell you," he said.

"Rupa is your ex-wife, she betrayed you and took over your business entirely.

She gave you drugs and made you believe that you were running your business. She made you sign on all the powers of attorney and took over all the businesses.

She put bangles in your hands.

The steel ones.

You faced the worst movements with her. I pity you, my boy," he said, with pain in his voice.

"Where can I find her?" I asked him.

"Santacruz," he said.

That British accent roamed in my mind.

I felt sad for a moment, but then I had to continue.

He told me that he could let me sleep in his apartment for a while since I looked tired. But I preferred to sleep on the streets.

Five days passed by.

I thought as if I had clinomania.

But I had to get up and catch a cab for Santacruz.

AGE 37

I took a cab, but I had no money; no money at all.
Only God knew how I was going to pay the taxi driver.
I told him directly that I don't have money.
"I know that," he told me.
"How?" I asked him.
"Does it matter?" he retorted.
It reminded me of that runner. I bent ahead to see his face,
and to my surprise, he was that runner himself. I was about to

tell him about my destination. But before I could do so, he shouted at the top of his voice,

"Santacruz, right?"

I was shocked that he knew my destination and asked him about it.

He reciprocated saying, "Just as I know you."

As I looked out of the window, I saw people running here and there.

While the poor children were begging on the streets, their rich counterparts were sipping chilled drinks.

I wondered about myself. Was I rich or poor, young or old, sad or happy, monster or an angel, whether I have been a good man or a bad man, did I have children; my own children?

Had I experienced happiness or sorrow?

These questions kept hammering my mind as if somebody was punching me on my head. I felt bad; terribly bad. The cab stopped.

I yelled at him,

"Are you alright? Why did you stop the cab?"

"Because we have arrived sir," he said.

"So why do you run?" I asked him as I got out of the car.

"Because everyone runs," he smiled and looked to his right.

I followed his gaze, and a towering building drew my attention. It had a big hoarding of Rupa Airlines. I walked across to the building and walked through the glass door, leading to the office of Rupa Airlines.

Without realising what I was doing, I asked the girl behind the inquiry counter about Rupa, as if I was aware that the office was headed by Rupa. The girl asked me to wait and pointed to a fluffy chair for me to settle in. In my eagerness to meet Rupa, I lost track of time. I had waited for two hours, and the waiting was frustrating.

Suddenly, the glass door opened and a tall sensuous lady walked through it, with speed that may have put a cheetah to shame.

She stopped in her stride when she saw me and stared at me with her eyes wide open. Her stare was scary, something I had not seen earlier.

She shouted at the girl at the reception, "Let this man wait for four hours if he wants."

Keeping her pace, she walked through another door, which I presumed led to her cabin.

After four hours she called me in.

As I walked into her magnificent cabin, she said, "So Harish, you're interested? Wow, thank you so much."

"Yes," I replied.

"You idiot," she snarled.

"Why what happened?" I questioned.

"You fired five of our best pilots. As a result, 1000 employees left the job."

I was shocked. "If I fired five employees, how the hell did the 1000 employees leave the job?" I asked

"Psychology!" she said, "When you fired the best employees, the rest knew their worth and followed them."

Then came the most anticipated question.

"Do you still love me?"

I reciprocated saying "What do you want me to say?"

"Whatever your heart feels," she said in soft voice.

That voice, which had a longing to hear a positive response, made my heart skip a beat and later started beating faster.

"You were the CEO, Harish. CEO. Look at yourself now. Look at yourself, you fool. What have you done to yourself? You were a sweetheart. The best man I knew. You have ruined your life as well as mine. You idiotic person," she said in anguish.

"Sorry," I muttered and repeated, "I'm sorry."

"What now?" she asked.

"You tell me, what now?" I reciprocated.

"Get out, Harish. Go spend some time with our daughter. She will tell you the rest of your story."

"I already met Nazuk."

"Not Nazuk," she said.

"Then who?" I asked.

"Are you really bothered to know?" she questioned.

"Yes, obviously," I said.

"Her name is Radha. our child Radha. Take this money and go find her. She lives in Thakur Complex. She always remembers you, always tries to find you. She looks for you in every man she meets. It's time Harish that you go and meet her. She always remembers you, asks for you, begs for you, prays for you, tries to find you, but the man who is already lost in himself can never be found."

I did not realise that tears rolled down my cheeks as I heard Rupa speak.

"Go, Harish meet your real daughter," she said in a pleading voice.

I embarked on my next journey.

AGE 36

Took a cab again. I was crying a lot; way too much. I did not know how time passed by, but I had reached Thakur Complex.

I reached her place and met her there.

To my utter surprise, the man who opened the door was the runner, the cabbie. He turned out to be her care-taker.

She was emotionally weak. 'Mentally challenged was not the right word or was it?' I questioned myself.

"Welcome," he said, "I knew you would come here."

When I approached her, and I touched her shoulder, she shrugged and started laughing.

"Why are you laughing?" I asked.

"You look familiar to the person from my childhood," she said and started drawing again.

I again tried to show sympathy, but she bit my hand.

I got too agitated, and I got up to step out, but the runner-cabbie caught my hand and forced me to sit down.

"Sit down pal; I want to show you a photograph," he said.

He then showed me a photograph of her and me.

That photograph took me into a flashback. A flashback full of memories. I was very eager to meet her as I left the office of Rupa Airlines; extremely eager.

She was the little love of my life; my angel. My everything.

Everything of hers depended on me.

On me, alone.
But then I had to leave.
Leaving that place, was the only option.
My heart had overtaken greed.
Love was lost.
And my job package.
Felt everything to me.
She wept as she held my hand.
She locked the doors of the gate in order to prevent me from going.

"Don't leave me, daddy. I love you," were her words.

She kept repeating her words, but I was too greedy.

I wanted to reach for more.

Today, I came back for her, to the same house where I had left her.

She had stayed here for her entire life.

But now she was different.

The runner-cabbie told me, "You have lost her, and she has lost herself. It's time you meet her real mother."

"Rupa right?"

"No," he said with a smile.

"Go meet her," he said.

I was startled when he told me that her name is Nahima and that she lives in Bandra East.

AGE 35

This was so insane, extremely insane, I thought.

Now I have to go and find her biological mother.

God knows what she would say now.

I saw a glow party being held in the middle of the street.

I thought they had musicomania or maybe they were just high on weed or some other kind of drugs.

My eyes became soaked in sleep.

"I was bloating."

Repeat.

"I was bloating."

She was Nahima, who had mothered by daughter—our biological daughter.

The woman I made love to. The woman who knew the secrets of this chapter of my life. The woman I was in love with, she was my love, whom I had forgotten.

"Has she forgotten me?" I wondered.

Will she remember me? Will she recognise me? Will she tell me my story? Will she even bother to talk to me? These questions were on my mind.

It got tough.

Extremely tough.

My mind was blocked.

I didn't know where I was going. I reached her home. It was a short ride. It seemed to be the shortest ride possible.

It was a skyscraper.

I used the intercom at the gate to connect to her apartment and ask for Nahima.

There was a long queue.

The watchman told me to wait for eight hours.

Two hours passed by; a woman signalled to me from the 15th floor.

She waved at me, and it was like a green signal to let me in.

I was immediately allowed to go in. I entered the lift, and I could see everybody staring at me.

When I stared back in annoyance, they looked away and giggled as if I had cracked the most spectacular joke of the decade.

I reached the 15th floor. Just as I was going to ring the bell, she opened the door.

She asked me, in the sternest tone possible, "So Harish, what brings you here? Do you need any financial assistance? Do you need some favours? Tell me, Harish what brings you here?"

She fired her questions one after the other.

"May I answer?" I reciprocated.

She said, "No, not at all. Just shut up and listen."

I said, "Alright."

"You are the most idiotic man in the universe. I can't believe you did this. You were so harsh, Harish, why did you do this to us?" I was shocked.

"Please relax," I said.

"We were so happy together. So extremely happy. We had a cute daughter. But you had other commitments. You left all of us. But before that, you harassed everybody in our family. Everybody," she said.

'Everybody' was the word that kept ringing on my mind.

"You subjected me to domestic violence. You beat our cute daughter. You had sex with the house-maid in my absence. You cruel man. No, you aren't a man, you are a monster," she said.

"Why don't you go and meet your therapist? He also guided you. Right?" she said in the most sarcastic way possible.

"Your therapist lives in Dadar. Go meet him and improve yourself. Start thinking for others too. Please Harish, grow up at some point in time."

She gave me a visiting card. It read.

Dr. Nasir, with a tagline 'Love yourself for what you are and others for what they are."

AGE 34

I continued my journey. It was too painful. I always wondered, "How cruel I have been."

Dr. Nasir, my therapist. Wow.

I continued my journey to this therapist. His office and home was in Khar.

Because he was living his dream.

The job of a therapist was the best in town I thought.

As I visited him, I got positive vibes from him. He was an elderly man. His aura was charismatic. His voice displayed kindness. His wall was lined up with multiple degrees and certificates. Among these was The Best Therapist Award by the Psychiatrist Association of India. He was a lover of nature.

He was a good guide, the best guide that anyone could find. He was loving and caring. His age was 81 years.

The whole world knew the secret behind his smile because he knew about life more than anybody else.

He was a charming man. His soul was pure, purer than mineral water.

His eyes.

All of this

Seeing him once again, I was reminded of that year. The year when I became greedy. When I became the greediest man on the planet. I wanted money. I went into drugs.

I had overcome with lust. I stopped believing in love. Love was the last thing on my priority list.

I went into the betrayal mode. I betrayed everyone I knew. Dr. Nasir was the only man I trusted. He was a mastermind. He helped me play the game. He showed me the path to success. Success was the only thing I wanted, and it was the only thing I saw.

I loved what I did, and that was to irritate people.

"Are we done, Harish?" he smiled.

I said, "Yes, sir" and I decided to sign off. Just as I was signing off, he asked me a very interesting question. "Do you still love her?"

"Who?" I asked

"Her," he said again

I got too agitated. But I tried to maintain my composure. I took a deep breath and said, "Can you please tell me?"

"Yes, wait," he said.

He made me wait for two hours, after which he said, "Asha. Your true love, Asha. Go to town; you will find Asha there.

"I hope I don't find *nirasha* in Asha," I thought to myself.

As I signed off, I introspected my cruelty.

AGE 33

I took a cab to town.

As I reached there, three things struck me:

1. Life isn't fair.
2. Life is good when you care.
3. Life is worst when you care the most.

There was a very old voice in my head which said such things. It was a motherly voice.

I ran helter-skelter, trying to find Asha. I found her after two hours.

I noticed a board on a building with the name Asha Foundation on it

As I entered inside, I felt I had entered spirituality. There was a positive aura in that room. An aura like no other.

An aura of hope.

An aura of freedom.

An aura of love and affection.

An aura of extreme well being.

An aura to remember for the way it is.

An aura to go with the flow.

An aura dressed in a white saree finally came out of the room.

She was a motherly figure. On seeing her, I remembered that she had told me those magical words of love and affection, the secret of life.

She held my hand and took me to a spiritual room and helped me sit down.

She then made me join my hands and asked me to focus. She made me remember this year. This year was full of peace; full of freedom; full of prosperity of the soul and not of money.

It made me a great guy.

From my soul.

My heart blossomed. I understood that I had come here for a reason. This year was full of prayers. Full of hope and wisdom. Full of dreams to win the world. Detaching myself, understanding my soul, detoxifying myself, understand myself, loving myself, proving myself, looking ahead in life, when things fell apart.

This year was spiritual, the best year of my life. The year when I found my soul. The year in which I found my life to be a better place to live in.

The love of my life was to love myself, for who I was and not for who I was not.

She told me to go to a municipal school in Vile Parle (West).

There I could unravel the rest of my story.

AGE 32

I started my journey to Vile Parle. Once there, I saw the municipal school. It was a municipal school like an ancient house. It was rickety, but the children inside were very enthusiastic about education.

They loved what they did. They were playful. They were the new souls who entered the world.

They were too honest.

They seemed to love their life.

The best part about them was that they never cribbed.

They took life as it came to them because it was new to them.

They were the children of God.

The children loved the gift of life.

Looking at the children, I remembered that I was a teacher, yes, a teacher. I taught in this school.

I was a teacher with too much self-esteem. A teacher, who gave life to the students. A teacher, who taught ethics. A teacher, who taught about good touch and bad touch. A teacher, who gave a lot of love to his students.

There I saw a super scared girl. There was a pain in her eyes. The pain in her eyes took me into a journey of insecurity. It reminded me of something, something which can never be forgotten.

It took me back to the most disgusting year of my life.

AGE 31

This was a very horrible year. I had sexually assaulted the girl. Shouted at her. Beaten her; raped her.

These were the so many sins committed by me. I was literally a monster. A monster. I repeat.

The poor girl, she was so small so tender, so cute.

But I couldn't curtail the monster in me. I became a very cruel man. A very insane man. The most horrible one from the lot. Humanity had switched definitions in this year.

This girl was an orphan, so I adopted her.

She was the victim of the pressure of work I was facing at the office.

She was living the most horrible dream of her life. The most horrible dream. She regretted being with me. She wanted to go to school.

So, when I was done with her , I sent her to this school where she could learn.

What an irony, I taught ethics in this school.

To keep a watch on her.

Then I realised that I used to live in Malad (East).

I had to find an end to this misery.

This pain, which I got to know.

I had to find out what went so wrong with my character that I became like this. This was an insane journey, but a promising one, indeed.

AGE 30

I reached Malad (East). It gave me a sense of satisfaction when I saw the place where I lived.

I stood there for five hours as people passed by.

I continued to stand, even as the hours ticked by. Seeing the people passing by, I felt they were like wind, you can feel it, it comes and goes, but you cannot hold it. But you remain where you are, like a milestone.

I entered the house, where I used to stay earlier. It was occupied by a couple of tenants. They ignored me for some apparent reason.

Apparently, life was not fair. Was it? I asked myself.

My own place and yet, my own people aren't allowing me inside it. "Why?" I wondered. These tenants were my distant relatives.

After a couple of hours, they started interacting with me. They told me how I let them stay in this house. But I was a very weird person. I abandoned them completely. I was a psychopath. I wanted a hold on to everybody; I wanted to control them. I always wanted to be a ruler, a ruler of the world.

But I had no control over myself.

I was an animal, who wanted to become strong. Strong in order to have a better hold on more people. For a human being that could be achieved by growth, so I left these people behind in order to grow.

"So, did you become a ruler?" a giggling boy asked.

"I don't remember," I said.

"I came back to recall the same!" I exclaimed.

I recalled that I ate here. Played with the children of the house. Danced. Drank alcohol. Loved life. Loved the people around me.

In a small one bedroom-hall-kitchen, I found love.

The children were cute. The people were cute.

"I found love here," I said to myself.

A monster like me finding love was like finding an oasis in a desert.

Lost love found.

I always dreamt of being settled in a place. Only God knows why I left such a divine temple of happiness.

I was there for 50 days. I remembered each and everything.

Everything that I did here now echoed in my mind.

I recalled my disasters and my blunders.

It all became right when I came back to this place.

I found love in the souls of the people, whom I had hurt.

"It's time for you to leave, Harish," the eldest man in the house told me.

"Why?" I asked.

"Because it is time," he replied.

"Go and find about your schooling," he said.

"Ok, sir," I told him.

"But where can I find that out?" I queried.

"Goregaon East," he said.

"Alright," I said and asked if I could leave.

He smiled and said, "Yes, you may!"

AGE 29

I continued my journey and reached Goregaon East.

There I saw my school. It was a very great school. It was an elitist school. I heard the students speaking with a British accent.

It was an International Board school. My parents must have been rich; I thought because the fee structure was too exorbitant. Extremely exorbitant, I thought.

Strangely the watchman at the gate greeted me with a smile as I entered the school premises. I found it strange that he did not stop me from entering the school premises.

Generally, security personnel are very strict. Extremely strict. But this man was kind. Extremely kind. I don't know why.

"I have always missed you," he said.

"Thanks," I said.

That sounded gay though.

My heart sank. Somehow that man was related to me in some manner, I thought. As I entered the school, where I had studied, I recalled everything.

I had studied ten classes in this school. I had a hunger for learning. I loved reading. Books were my best friends. Best friends, I believe.

Calculators were my second-best friends.

People were tools, tools that I used to pass every class.

Education was important to me in life.

I always believed people were mad and I was always right on each and every matter. I was every teacher's pet.

Every student disliked me because I was too elder to them.

I always topped the class; each and every time.

I used to sit on the first bench. I understood the subjects taught and took notes properly.

The lazy students always wanted copies of my notes, but I kept them at bay by all possible means.

They weren't as hardworking as me, that was always my belief. There was no substitute for hard work. Other people used to fall in love, while I used to be engrossed in my books.

When I slept, I used my books as my pillow.

I did not believe in love.

I was all set to conquer the world.

AGE 28

I had a little secret. A very little one. I had a crush on the high school principal's daughter. She used to study with me.

My policy of not giving my notes to anyone was broken only in the case of one person, and that was her.

I used to call her my sister in order to camouflage my relationship with her from the principal.

Her name was Kasak. She was the most popular girl in school. She was chubby and had curly hair. She was beautiful.

Her favourite sport was swimming.

She was a world-class swimmer. She had won international gold medals in swimming. But yet so down to earth.

She loved life, and I loved her.

I was scared to express to her my feelings for her, worried that she would stop talking to me.

She was very friendly, and she had a vast friends' circle.

There was a rumour in school that she was already married.

AGE 27

I saw Kasak for the first time while I was doing my homework. She was with a guy. The guy was very good looking and charming.

He was 6 feet and 2 inches tall and had a fair complexion.

He had worn a t-shirt, but I assume that he had six-pack abs.

I was not gay, but yes, I wished strongly that he was her brother.

I continued my hard studies, and she soon noticed me. We became friends and developed the brother-sister relationship or the best friend-best friend relationship I felt.

The entire school tried to get my notes from her, but she was a very loyal friend. She never betrayed me. She kept the notes to herself. She was a very curious creature.

She always had doubts, very stupid doubts but I was forced to ask smart questions.

She was very temperamental, in short, she was insane.

AGE 26

I came back into reality.

Age 26. This year was a very dry year. By dry I mean,

I never drank. I was childish. I concentrated only on my studies, without being distracted by anything else. I focused only on my studies.

Many sensuous girls tried to approach me for friendship, but I had double thoughts that they contacted me for my notes.

I was worried that their boyfriends, who were tough, would beat me up if they found me speaking to these girls. So, I did not talk to any girl in my school. I was the most silent person in the school and was always engrossed in my books.

My books were my Bible, Bhagvad Gita, and Quran. I loved each and every book of mine.

People of my age were in love with members of the opposite gender, but I was in love with my books.

AGE 25

This year was the reason why the previous year was so dry. I harassed a girl by mistake. By mistake is not a good phrase to use. But yes. I did become a victim of lust. It destroyed my academics that year. I was debarred from school. I was ruined.

The year was a wet year, the year when everything went wrong. I stopped studying. I was sent to jail. I had a bad name in school. My goodwill was destroyed. Nobody spoke to me. I was the blacklisted person in the society.

AGE 24

I again came back to reality. This year was the reason why I became so cruel and why I harassed a girl. I had a fight with my dad on the issue of ethics. I saw him beating mom. My mom was a homemaker.

He beat me a lot when I protested at the way he was treating my mother. I was agitated that he treated my mother badly and was furious that he beat me for my protest. I wanted to take revenge for his behaviour.

I did outside the house, what he did inside.

My dad was merely a watchman standing at the gate. He requested the top authorities to take me in.

They were reluctant, but they took me in, and that was because my father worked there as a watchman for the past 30 years.

AGE 23

I was a very shy boy, extremely shy. I attribute my shyness to my father's sternness.

His strict attitude made me completely opposite.

I was a contrast to my father. A completely different person.

But I had seen the dust, and I had seen the sky.

Because of him.

He was very kind-hearted. He was always right in any decision he took, which I realise now.

I was preparing for military school, but I was too weak, too frail, too skinny, extremely weak minded.

Needless to say, I was rejected by the military. I tried hard, but I never got in. As an alternative, I got into this prestigious school.

AGE 22

My grandmother expired. It was the most devastating moment of my life. Her death came as a shock to me. Everybody at my place was in grief.

Death was the most horrifying thing that I had ever faced. Grief was in the air. It was disastrous.

I had seen my grandmother as the happiest person in the world.

She was evergreen.

She was a very spiritual person and as a result, contended. Her smile was priceless.

She was uneducated, but she had the knowledge of the world, she had wisdom.

She died as she lived--in happiness.

AGE 21

When grandmother fell sick, my mom stopped her household work and started taking care of her.

My dad and my grandmother did not ever share a good rapport.

But at this time, I saw that they shared a special bond. I started understanding the concept of caring. Till now I had seen the people in the house fighting with each other, like animals. I had not seen this kind of love in the family; I have seen even animals exhibit love towards each other and towards human beings. But, the people in the house were different, they did not see eye to eye.

I saw my parents take care of my grandmother and saw the bonding between the two of them, love got a meaning in the house. It made me have faith in love.

Love consumed me even before I met Kasak. Life became wonderful even during the moment of crisis. I saw inevitable affection between these people.

My dad used to work for seven hours at a salary of Rs 4,000.

But later he started working part-time on a salary of Rs 2,000 so that he could come home early to take care of his mother-in-law.

AGE 20

I was a young bud. I was a new flower without any immorality in me.

I did not know about betting games or about drugs.

I did not raise my hands at anyone.

I did not do anything wrong, but I did something right, which was to obey my parents.

I did not tell lies at home. If I liked a girl, I mentioned that at home and my parents would laugh and make fun of me, leaving me embarrassed and blushing. My cheeks would become redder than a red rose.

When it came to human relations, I was always neutral. People used to come to me in order to resolve a fight as they looked at me as a fight solver; as an angel.

The son of a watchman, yet a son of God. The god, who saved me from everything, from all the immorality in the world. The god saved me from the sins in the world. He stopped me from doing illegal things.

AGE 19

This was the last of my teenage years. I loved chewing gum. I wore low waist jeans; so low that my underwear would be visible. I wore a cap, with the logo of my favourite international band. I used to walk with hands in my pockets.

I used to look up at the sky and wish that one day I would become so rich that I could take care of my father very well because, after all, he gave me everything that I wanted. He gave me good clothes to wear even though his clothes were torn. I loved him for what he was. I respected him. I saw him as a man who was always standing; a man who was always there when I needed a shoulder to cry on; a man who was always by my side when I felt low; a man who loved and hated me at the same time. He taught me important life lessons, which I am able to remember quickly now.

He told me, "Always be true to yourself, no matter how badly other people treat you. Love yourself for who you are and not for who you are not."

He was Dr. Nasir's best friend.

AGE 18

To me, this was a marathon year. I ran a lot of marathons, so to say. Every time I ran, I felt that I was running a marathon. Some of these were because of the fear that I carried. This may sound hilarious, but it is true.

Once, I ran away from home. On another occasion, I ran away from my tuition classes.

Instead of being upset with me and firing me, my father told me to run for a good cause. So, I started running for a good cause.

I ran 50 marathons in this 18th year of my life.

I was named 'The marathon boy' by the Daily Times magazine.

When I used to walk on the streets, people used to mock at me saying, "Why aren't you running, marathon boy?" I would laugh along with them. They laughed at my running, and I laughed at their query. Little did they knew about me. I hated people, but I loved my life.

The way running made sense, nothing else did.

AGE 17

I suddenly started growing tall. I became the tallest person of my age in the housing society where I lived.

My height made me feel that I was getting a view from above, a feeling I loved.

I gave people an inferiority complex.

Children, who were short, used to cry to their mothers, wanting to grow as tall as me. But there was no possibility in that. I was still the tallest.

I was childish, but yes, I loved being that way. These were my growing years. I used to tease other children, "shorty, shorty."

I was an epitome of confidence. The best part was that I used to feel that I am on the terrace and people lived on the ground floor. They always used to look up at me, so my height was a great advantage to me.

Even if I did wrong stuff, people had my back.

Which was very wrong but yes it was even right.

It was a two-way process.

I did wrong.

And I did right.

But I did not have double standards. I had leveraged upon my good habits and glorified them.

I became very famous in the society.

AGE 16

I saw a girl. A girl, who was very familiar. We both looked at each other, and our hearts met.

Our souls touched.

Infatuation, I heard. I felt it was immature love.

Yes, with some research I understood that her name was 'Kasak.'

We played House, where children play the role of adults in the house. We used to hold hands in the garden. We switched roles while playing house. She became the husband, and I became the wife.

As it is, I was like a girl, and she was like a guy.

She was more dominant, and I was not.

AGE 15

I was a good boy. Extremely good. I loved life the way it came.

I was my mother's *laadla*. (Mother's favourite)

Life was cute, and so were the people around me.

An uncle used to come home. He was used to giving us several sweets. He used to be in the army; I guess that was the reason why father wanted me to join the army.

That man was stern. He used to tell us interesting stories about his adventures in the army and how he walked out alive from each and every endeavour he took charge of.

He was a great man. He was a great guide. He always loved our country and wanted all of us to do the same.

His one lower limb was missing, as he lost it in a recent adventure fight.

But he would walk as if he had both his legs intact. He would be ever smiling, as he lived life like the way he wanted to and not as how others wanted him to.

He was an extremely nice person.

.

AGE 14

This was a very tragic year. The year when my father fell sick. He could not go to work, and all our sources of income were clearly shut.

We didn't have money even to pay our electricity bills.

Doctors came in every day, and we didn't have anything to pay them. But these doctors were generous. They did this for free. These doctors respected their profession. They treated my dad with love and care and thanks to them soon he was fine.

"It was a miracle!" one of the doctors said.

He had second level cancer, and only 10 out of 1 billion people can survive this disease, the doctor told us.

My dad became fit and this year had a happy ending.

AGE 13

My teens had started, and the effects of puberty were visible on my face, with pimples. My face was covered with pimples. My face was so full of pimples that one could barely see my face.

My life was turning.

Life became weird. People used to laugh at me because my face had too many blisters.

They laughed at my face.

And I pitied their soul.

I pitied them. They were materialistic. They could see the beauty of the face, but not the beauty of the soul.

It was at this time that my life became good because I understood who my true friends were and who dummies were.

Who were so materialistic and who were true to me.

This year was a year where I could actually differentiate between good and bad. My face was like a report card, with bad marks and I was able to see everybody's reaction.

AGE 12

I was a football fanatic. I loved watching football even if the match was being telecast late in the night. It was so interesting.

I was keen on joining the local football club and practiced a lot for that. But, to my utter disappointment, I did not get selected. Obviously, I wasn't good enough.

My body was weak, but my mind was sharp. I got good grades in school. I had beauty in my brains, but my physique went for a toss. A complete toss.

I knew I was blessed. I loved myself for who I was and not for who I was not. These lines were continuously playing in my head.

I wanted to be in the team, but I only got to see the real team play.

AGE 11

Love had consumed me. This year was the most spectacular year of my life.

My father gave me Malgudi Days to read. I fell in love with those stories.

Those stories used to take me on trips, while sitting in my room.

Love consumed. Love for those stories, which R K Narayan wrote.

They inspired me in every way possible. Life became inspirational. I saw hope. I started day-dreaming.

I went into a cage with that book.

I found the stories to be sublime. It gave my life a motto. A dream. A dream to be conquered. A dream to be lived. A dream in every story I read. A dream for which I understood that I had to live.

AGE 10

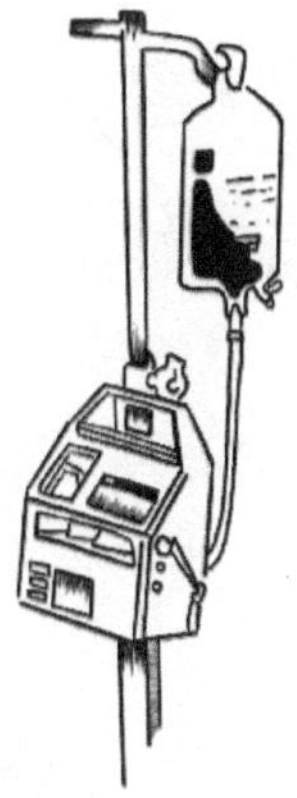

This year was a very disastrous year. The year in which everything went wrong. I met with a car accident, which meant that I faced a near death experience.

Life was cruel. I had no hope to live.

The noises became dizzy.

My father repeatedly told me, "You are going to be alright."

His voice became dizzy. I thought that I was going to die. I could hardly remember anything. I felt numb.

I had lost out on emotions. My mind went into a flashback mode, and in my sub-conscious mind, I started remembering the first decade of life.

AGE 09

I was too short. All my neighbours used to call me cutie-pie.

Cutie-pie was a nickname that I got.

From people in my society.

The worst part was that people compared me to their dog. Dog is considered the cutest animal they said.

But your child is cuter than our dogs, they would tell my parents and would laugh.

As they laughed, I could see their yellow teeth.

The bad odour from their mouth was a clear sign that they did not follow the habit of brushing their teeth regularly.

AGE 08

I found a very good friend. I would not call him my best friend. Because he was not perfect. I used to share everything with him.

His dad owned the local retail store.

We used to do a lot of cycling, rigorous cycling. We would fall down. Yet, we would get up and start cycling again.

Life was tough, but we both made it easy. We were like two parts of the same heart.

Life was the best when I was with him. His name was Raman.

Coincidently, he was Kasak's cousin brother.

AGE 07

This was the year when I met Raman. I had a craze for erasers. My mom always used to get me a box of erasers.

Once, I went out with my mom to get my favourite eraser, to a local retail shop and there he was with a couple of erasers.

He was juggling them. He was looking forward and juggling them.

His hand movements were in perfect harmony with the erasers, and his eyes were fixated on the wall ahead. It was as if he knew the timing of juggling the erasers.

As I continuously stared at him, he suddenly looked at me, and he lost control of his juggling.

All his erasers dropped down to the floor.

AGE 06

I was in primary school. I loved cream biscuits. I loved to run. I loved my parents.

When I saw fast cars, I always wanted to sit in them, but my mom always came in an autorickshaw to pick me up. I wondered why.

There was this thing I noticed. Even if we travelled on autos, she had a smile on her face, while the other children's parents who came in high-class premium cars were always worried, shouting and smoking cigarettes.

That's when I realised money couldn't buy real happiness.

AGE 05

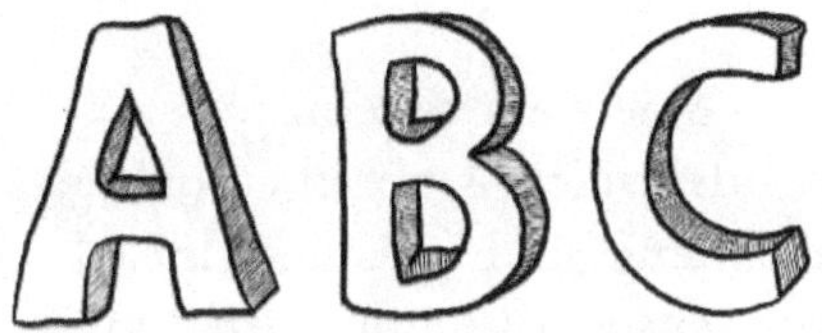

I started learning A,b,c. I started learning 1,2,3. I started learning how to walk. I started learning how to speak. I started learning to see things clearly with my big wide eyes.

AGE 04

The years to come were very dizzy.

I heard words which I couldn't understand. I slightly started understanding and grasping life. I slightly gained control over my senses. I slightly started understanding what was going around.

AGE 03

This year went by in sleeping and crying.

AGE 02

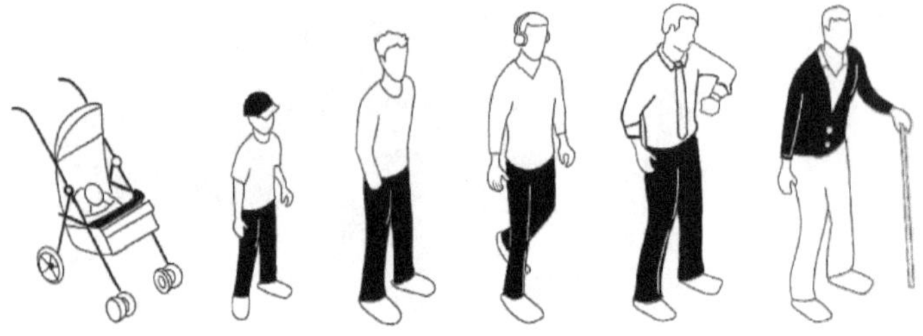

This year also went by in sleeping and crying.

AGE 01

My first birthday was celebrated in my mama shree's place.
Every relative came in to wish me.
I hardly knew anybody's name.
The truth was that I hardly knew mine.

AGE 00

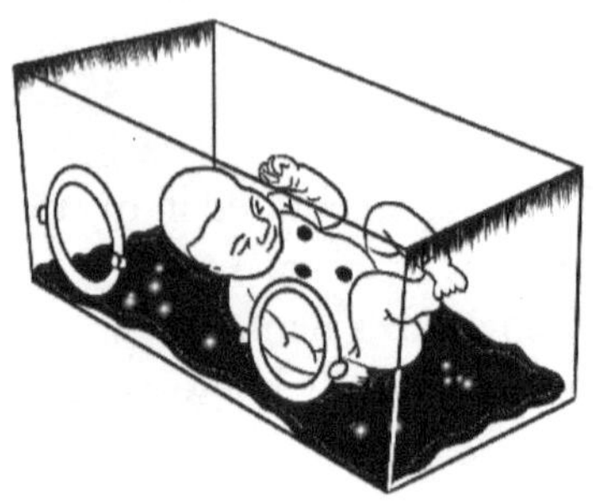

Incubator. I was a premature baby. The only thing I remembered was that I was running somewhere and I got hit by an auto.

Maybe I was a thief, or maybe I was trying to save my life. Not everything in life had a reason, did it?

EPILOGUE

Haria finally understood how his life went by.
He remembered everything that happened to him.
He was so busy making a living that he forgot to make a life.
Thus, during his golden jubilee year, he ended up all alone.
His life was tragic but yet an adventurous journey.
Nothing made sense.
At the end.
He tried to make sense of everything.
Be happy.
The only difference between learning and earning was of that of the missing "L" which stood for Love.